DATE DUE

PRINTED IN U.S.A.

Tiffany Stone

Rainbow Shoes

illustrations by **Stefan Czernecki**

Tradewind Books

Do you wear clothes?

You do?

We dedicate this book to **YOU.**

_____

Write your name here in colourful letters.

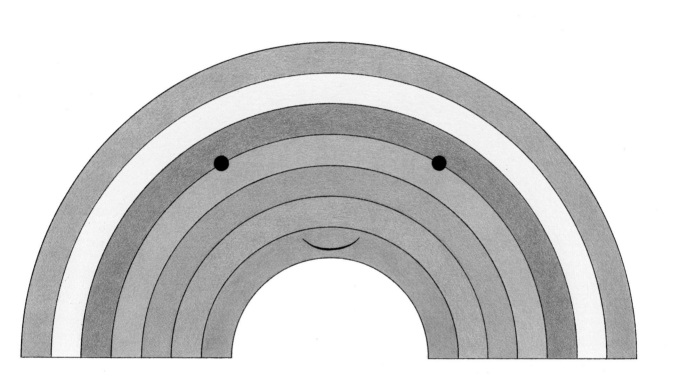

Rainbow Shoes

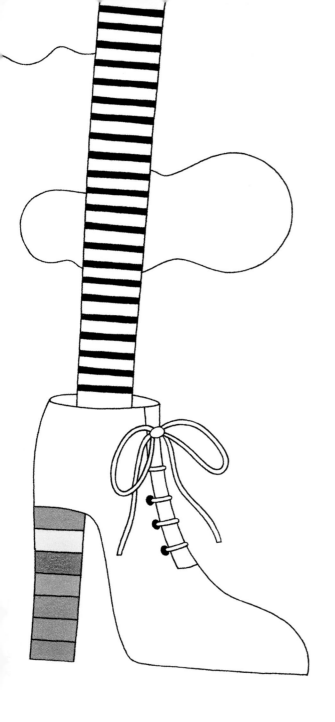

Got a case
of deep down blues?
Slip on a pair
of **rainbow** shoes!
Tie the laces
good and tight.
Those blues will vanish
out of sight.
Rainbow heels
will lift you high,
past grumpy clouds
to smiling sky.
And with each happy
step you take,
you'll leave a **rainbow**
in your wake.

Do Robots Wear Red Rubber Boots?

Do robots wear **red** rubber boots
to play out in the rain?
The answer's YES!
and—**beep beep**—NO!
and—**beep boop**—YES! again.
Cuz some bots do
and some bots don't
and some bots feel they *must*.
They worry if they go barefoot
their robot feet will rust.
They *always* wear their rubber boots.
Their boots are *always* **red**.
Red protects the very best.
That's what their mumbots said.

Orange Socks

Orange socks—yum.
Orange socks—nutritious.
Full of fibre, juicy good.
Orange socks—delicious!

Orange socks—pairs.
Orange socks—single.
So much fun upon the tongue.
Orange socks—tingle!

Orange socks—tight.
Orange socks—elastic.
Any shape and any size.
Orange socks—fantastic!

Orange socks—plain.
Orange socks—gourmet.
Keep your dryer happy. Feed it
orange socks—today!

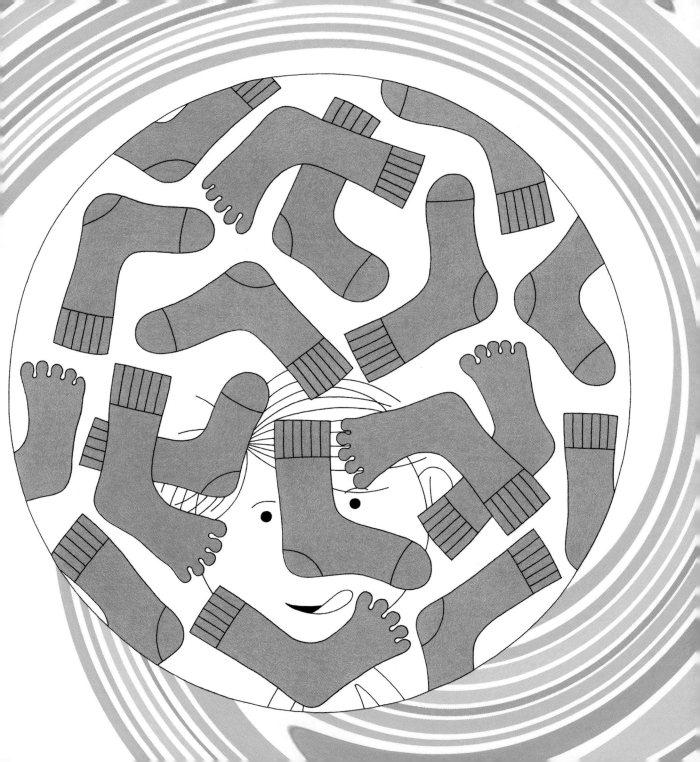

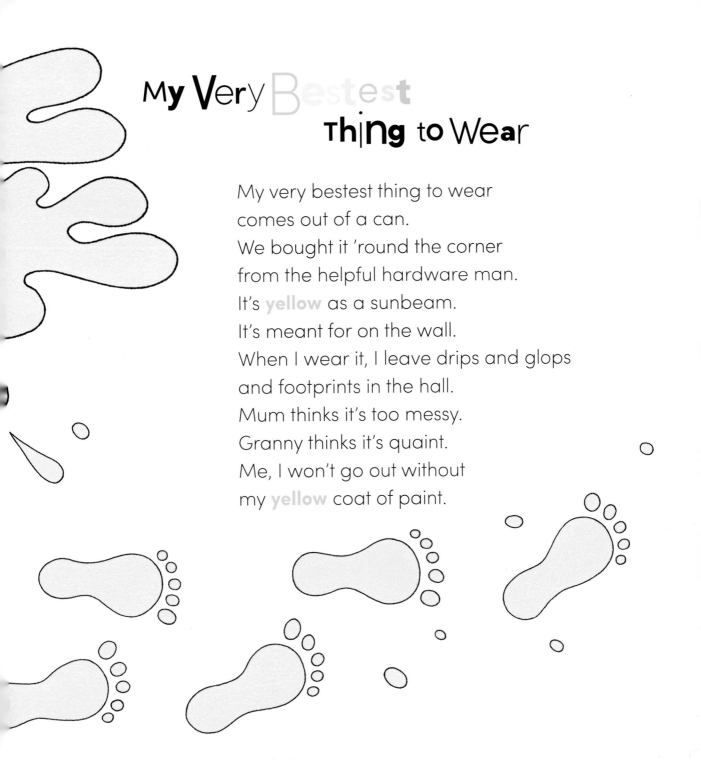

My Very Bestest Thing to Wear

My very bestest thing to wear
comes out of a can.
We bought it 'round the corner
from the helpful hardware man.
It's yellow as a sunbeam.
It's meant for on the wall.
When I wear it, I leave drips and glops
and footprints in the hall.
Mum thinks it's too messy.
Granny thinks it's quaint.
Me, I won't go out without
my yellow coat of paint.

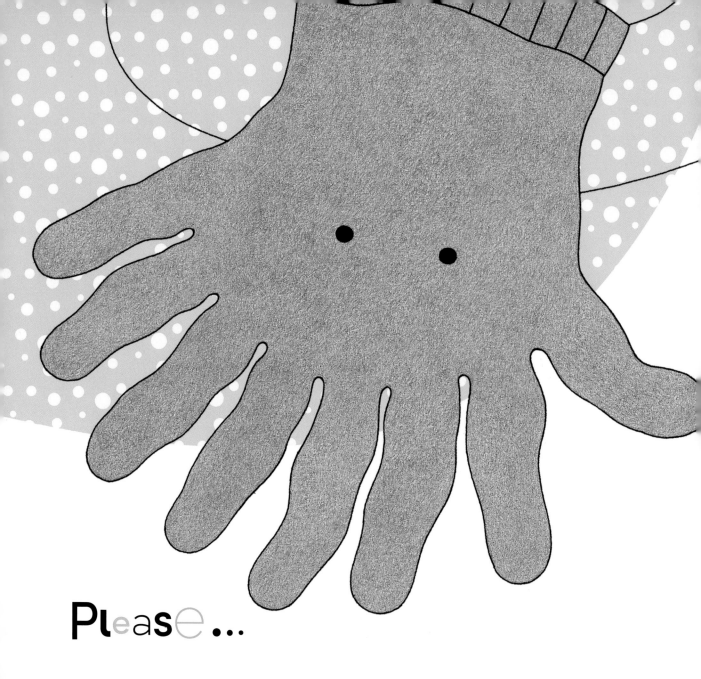

Please ...

Knit for me, with care and love,
one ghastly **green** and gruesome glove
for each and every hand that's mine,
which, at last count, was ninety-nine.
That's seven fingers and a thumb
times ninety-nine—and each one's numb!
It's draughty here beneath the bed.
I found a sock to warm my head.
But my poor hands are cold and bare.
Please knit with speed as well as care.
I've got a job to do tonight—
a tired child to give a fright—
which means it simply won't suffice
if all my hands are blocks of ice
since frozen fingers cannot creep
and scare that sweetheart far from sleep.

The Blues

I don't care what clothes I wear.
Why not? Because I've got **blue** hair.

In my ragged jeans, I'm a beauty queen
with my spiked-up hair dyed **ultramarine**.

Brother's hand-me-downs never make me frown.
Baby blue hair's better than a lace ball gown.

Even stains and holes don't bother me—no—
when my hair's streaked **cyan** or **indigo**.

Cobalt, **peacock**, **sapphire**, too.
I'm well-dressed cuz my hair is **blue**.

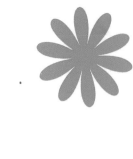

Purple Pants Poem

My pants, my pants,
my **purple** pants!
Put one leg on—
I do a dance.
The other—
see me strut and prance,
so *fancy*
in my **purple** pants.

I got them
from my crazy aunts—
my favourite ones—
who live in France.
My stylish moves
aren't happenstance.
There's *ooh la la*
sewn in my pants.

My pants, my pants,
my **purple** pants!
Wear something else?
No, not a chance!

What Do Pirates wear at Night?

What do pirates wear at night?
Pink pajamas. Arrrr, that's right!
Perfect for a pillow fight.

What do pirates wear for naps?
Pink pj's with feet 'n' flaps
'n' pockets for their treasure maps.

What do pirates wear to dream
of gold doubloons 'n' jewels that gleam?
"**Pink** pajamas!" they all scream.

Stars shine brightly overhead.
Tuck those pirates into bed!

The Top Thing in Toppers

Listen up, you young cowpokes.
Here's advice you should take.
Do not purchase a hat.
Get yer pans out 'n' bake.
Forget about felt
or the skin of some snake.
To top off yer head,
nothin' beats chocolate cake.
When you're out ropin' dogies
'n' can't take a break
but yer belly's a-grumblin'
'n' startin' to ache,
just bite the whole brim off
'n' freely partake
of the gooey **brown** goodness
of yer hat made of cake.

Polar Bear Buttons

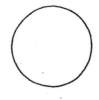

Big **black** buttons
are the very best
to button together
a polar bear's vest.
Bare bears shiver
in the cold white snow.
Buttoned-up bears
say, *"C'mon, let's go
to the Arctic Circle
and Iceberg Square,
the Beluga Triangle—
oops, not there—
but anywhere else
more than forty below.
Button those buttons.
Northward ho!"*

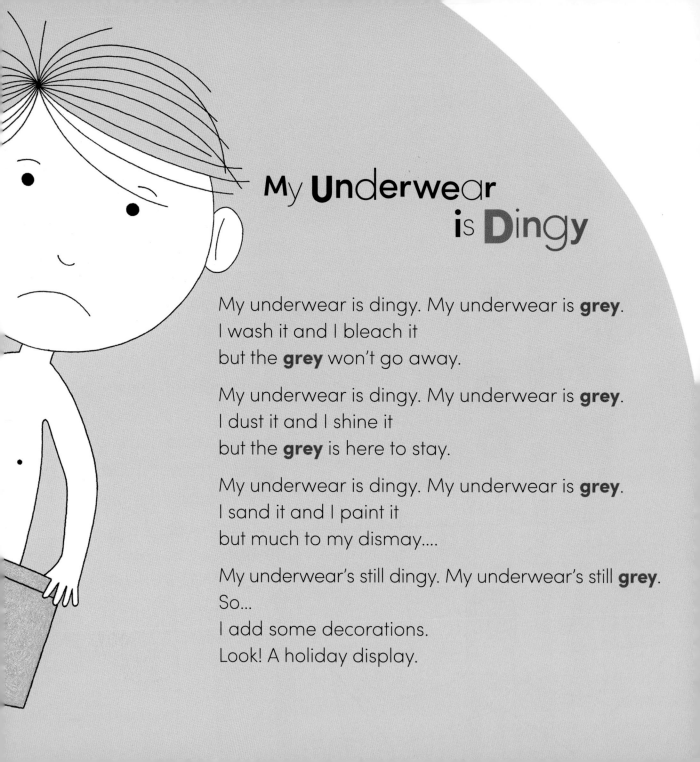

My **Un**derwe**ar** **is** **D**ingy

My underwear is dingy. My underwear is **grey**.
I wash it and I bleach it
but the **grey** won't go away.

My underwear is dingy. My underwear is **grey**.
I dust it and I shine it
but the **grey** is here to stay.

My underwear is dingy. My underwear is **grey**.
I sand it and I paint it
but much to my dismay....

My underwear's still dingy. My underwear's still **grey**.
So...
I add some decorations.
Look! A holiday display.

This Is Not Dad's Old Shirt

This is not Dad's old shirt,
boring white, fit just for work.
Look closely and you'll plainly see
all the things that it can be:

Flowing hair to swing and swish.
Wings for my pet flying fish.
An iceberg in a lava pool.
A Super cape that's supercool.
A tent for camping on the moon.
A creepy-crawly's huge cocoon.
A bandage for a bellyache.
A slice of puffy mushroom cake.
A screen to show a movie on.
A cloak that makes me—*poof*—all gone.

And gone is how I plan to stay
if you throw my not-a-shirt away!

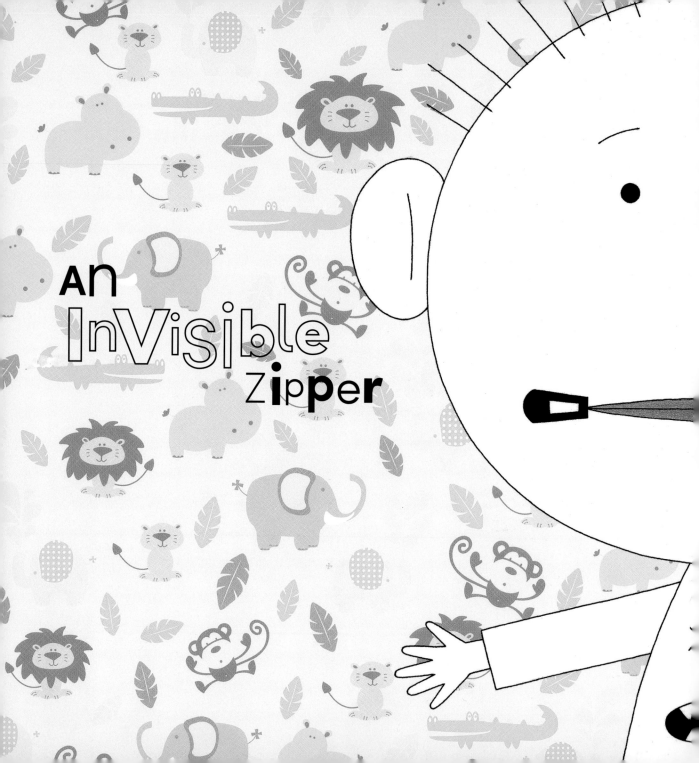

An InVisible Zipper

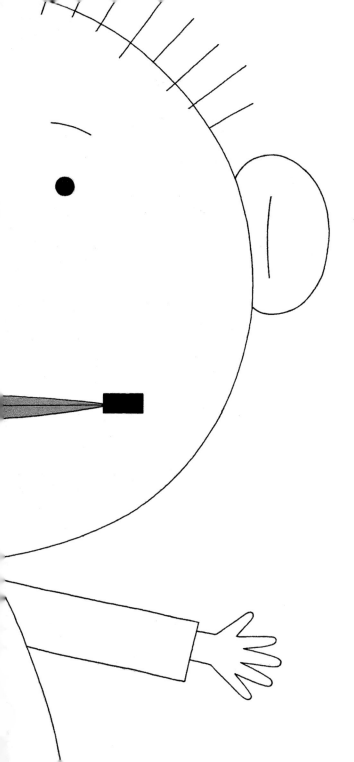

You—yes, YOU!
Don't you want to look hipper?
Everybody needs
an invisible zipper—
an all-purpose four-season
transparent gripper—
to hold on a horn
or attach a spare flipper,
disguise scary teeth,
plug a snout that's a dripper.
Buy one today!
You'll feel ten times more chipper
as soon as you own
an invisible zipper.

what if?

What if you woke up covered in spots—
bright candy-coloured polka dots—
not just a few but lots and lots?

Would you holler,
    "Get a doctor, please!
    An expert should examine these.
    I fear I've got a dread disease."

Or would you think,
    Hey, spots are chic!
    I hope they stick around a week.
    My polka-dotted skin's unique.

What would you do if you had dots?
Would you love the skin you were in—or not?

Published by Tradewind Books in Canada in 2012. **Text copyright** © **2012 Tiffany Stone** **Illustrations copyright** © **2012 Stefan Czernecki** Published in the US and the UK in 2013. All rights reserved. No part of this publication may be reproduced, stored in a retrieval system or transmitted, in any form or by any means, without the prior written permission of the publisher or, in the case of photocopying or other reprographic copying, a license from Access Copyright, Toronto, Ontario. The right of Tiffany Stone and Stefan Czernecki to be identified as the author and the illustrator of this work has been asserted by them in accordance with the Copyright, Design and Patents Act 1988. **Book design by Elisa Gutiérrez** Type is set in Sofia Pro. The artwork was created in ink, colour pencil and scrapbooking paper. 10 9 8 7 6 5 4 3 2 1 Printed in September 2012 by Friesens in Altona, Canada on FSC ® certified paper using vegetable-based inks

MIX
Paper from
responsible sources
FSC® C016245

LIBRARY AND ARCHIVES CANADA CATALOGUING IN PUBLICATION

Stone, Tiffany, 1967–
        Rainbow shoes / Tiffany Stone, Stefan Czernecki.

Poems.
ISBN 978-1-896580-85-2

        I. Czernecki, Stefan, 1946–   II. Title.

PS8637.T66R35 2012   jC811'.6   C2012-902207-1

Cataloguing and publication data available from the British Library

The publisher thanks the Government of Canada and Canadian Heritage
for their financial support through the Canada Council for the Arts, the
Canada Book Fund and Livres Canada Books. The publisher also thanks the
Government of the Province of British Columbia for the financial support
it has given through the Book Publishing Tax Credit program and the
British Columbia Arts Council.

Canada Council   Conseil des Arts
for the Arts   du Canada

BRITISH
COLUMBIA
ARTS COUNCIL